Antoine
master of the
Red sea

of
funny creatures

EVETTE SMITH

AuthorHouse™
1663 Liberty Drive
Bloomington, IN 47403
www.authorhouse.com
Phone: 833-262-8899

Because of the dynamic nature of the Internet, any web addresses or links contained in this book may have changed since publication and may no longer be valid. The views expressed in this work are solely those of the author and do not necessarily reflect the views of the publisher, and the publisher hereby disclaims any responsibility for them.

Any people depicted in stock imagery provided by Getty Images are models, and such images are being used for illustrative purposes only.
Certain stock imagery © Getty Images.

This book is printed on acid-free paper.

ISBN: 979-8-8230-2119-7 (sc)
ISBN: 979-8-8230-2118-0 (hc)
ISBN: 979-8-8230-2120-3 (e)

Library of Congress Control Number: 2024901594

Print information available on the last page.

Published by AuthorHouse 01/25/2023

authorHOUSE®

Antoine
master of the
Red sea
of funny creatures

Once upon a time, in the quiet little town of RedSeaville, three kids named Antoine, Tinkie, and Tashia lived. Antoine and Tinkie were brothers, always full of energy and positivity. Tashia was their shy little sister, but she had an incredible gift: she had binocular eyesight! She could see far and wide, much further than anyone else in RedSeaville. She also had a remarkable chair that could fly! Antoine was blessed with a super shield that had a cellphone, computer, and a sword. The shield serves to guide them all across the Red Sea and on land.

One sunny day, Antoine and Tinkie went on a journey across the Read Sea, while Tashia decided to visit the beach. The sand was warm beneath Tashia's feet as she strolled along the shore. Tashia couldn't help but be drawn to the sand, so she sat down near the water's edge, with her sand pail, special shovel and her flying super chair parked nearby.

With her binocular eyesight, Tashia noticed something sparkling in the sand. She reached down and uncovered a beautiful baby starfish and seashells. Excitedly, she showed it to Antoine and Tinkie, who admired its intricate patterns.

Tashia's eyes sparkled with delight as she had an idea. She grabbed her pail and shovel and started building a sandcastle. With each scoop of sand, her castle grew taller and more magnificent.

Antoine and Tinkie were amazed at Tashia's creativity. Antoine used his super shield's computer to search for starfish seashells to decorate the sandcastle while Tinkie gathered driftwood to make a flag.

As Tashia continued to mold the sand, she couldn't resist the urge to hop into her flying super chair. With a press of a button, the chair slowly lifted off the ground, floating just above the sand. Tashia giggled with joy as she flew in circles around her sandcastle, feeling like she was soaring through the sky.

The children laughed and played, their imaginations taking them to far-off lands and exciting adventures. Tashia's super chair added a touch of magic to their beach day, making it even more special.

As the sun began to set, casting a warm orange glow over the beach, the children admired their sandcastle masterpiece. It stood tall and proud, a testament to their kinship and creativity. They knew that even though the tide would wash it away, the memories they made that day would stay with them forever.

Hand in hand, Antoine, Tinkie, and Tashia walked back home, their hearts full of joy and the sand still clinging to their shoes. They couldn't wait to share their beach day stories with their families and dream about their next adventure together.

And so, in the land of RedSeaville, the three children continued to explore the world around them, finding magic in the simplest of things and spreading love and friendship wherever they went.

One sunny afternoon, Tashia, with her binocular eyesight, spotted some strange creatures emerging from the sea. They were the Sandball Man, the Sand Monkey, and a bunch of sea creatures. They looked a bit scary but also quite lost.

"We need to help them," Antoine declared. He was always the brave one. Tinkie, ever the loyal brother, nodded in agreement.

Since Tashia was shy, she chose to help from her super flying chair, scouting from above and giving directions to Antoine and Tinkie. Antoine, armed with his super shield, approached the group of sea creatures, while Tinkie stayed close to his side.

Suddenly, the Sandball Man threw a ball of sand towards them. Antoine, with lightning-fast reflexes, used his super shield to deflect it. The Sand Monkey, seeing this, started to throw sand balls too!

But Antoine and Tinkie didn't fight back. Instead, Antoine used his super shield's cellphone to call the Sandball Man. "We don't want to fight," he said. "We want to be friends. Maybe we can help you find your way back home."

Sandball Man and the Sand Monkey were surprised. They had been lost and scared too, and they had only thrown sand balls because they didn't know what else to do. Hearing Antoine's offer, they agreed to stop the sand fight.

From her super chair, Tashia used her binocular eyesight to lead the way back to the sea. The sea creatures, Sandball Man, and Sand Monkey thanked their new friends and promised to visit again, but peacefully this time.

From that day forward, the children of RedSeaville knew they could face any challenge with courage and kindness. Antoine, Tinkie, and Tashia had not only won a battle, but they had also won some very unusual friends. And they realized that sometimes, the best way to fight is to make friends instead.

And so, the three friends continued their exciting adventures, always ready to lend a helping hand, armed with Antoine's super shield, Tashia's binocular eyesight and flying chair, and their unending courage and kindness.

Printed in the United States
by Baker & Taylor Publisher Services